Careers-Day Surprise

Contents

Written by Alexandra Boow
Illustrated by Trevor Pye

Worried

Fiona was worried. Today was careers day, and she had to bring one of her parents to school to talk to her class about their job.

Fiona had asked her mother, but she couldn't get the day off work. So Fiona's father had said he would do it. When she asked him what he was going to talk about, he said it would be a surprise. Fiona just hoped he wouldn't bore her class too much.

All the other parents who had talked to her class seemed to have such exciting jobs. Sam's mother was a nurse in a trauma unit, and she told them what it was like to try and help people who had been in an accident.

Keally's father was a police officer. He told them how the police collected evidence at a crime scene. That had been really interesting.

"Fiona," her father called out, "it's time to go."

Fiona picked up her bag and walked out to the car. She dragged her feet. It was going to be a long day.

Fiona listened to the car radio on the way to school and tried not to think about anything.

"Don't look so worried, Fiona," her father said. "I think everyone is going to have a great day."

"I'm not worried," lied Fiona. "I think you'll do just fine."

She smiled at him, but she could see he didn't believe her. So she made a bigger effort and stretched her smile as wide as it would go.

"OK, you can relax now," he laughed, "I believe you."

Fiona couldn't help worrying. She trusted her father, but she would feel better if she knew what part of his job he was going to talk about. If he'd asked her, she could have told him what kind of things her class would be interested in. But he hadn't asked.

When they got to school, Fiona helped her father carry some boxes into the classroom. One of them was very heavy. Fiona hoped it wasn't full of boring, old rocks!

"Thanks, Fiona," said her father when they'd taken everything into the classroom. "I think that's all. Why don't you go over and say hello to Sheena while I finish setting up."

Sheena was Fiona's best friend. As Fiona wandered over to her, she saw that Sheena seemed very interested in the things Fiona's father had in the boxes.

"Hi, Fiona", said Sheena. "Your dad's brought enough stuff with him!"

"I know," said Fiona. "Don't ask me what it's for. Dad wouldn't tell me. He just said he wanted it to be a surprise."

"I think it'll be great," Sheena stated loyally.

"I hope you're right," replied Fiona.

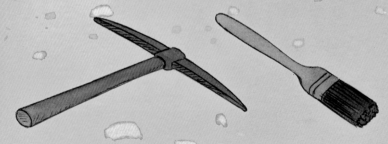

The Special Guest

Just as they finished talking, Mr. Moore, the teacher, came in and spoke to Fiona's father. The school bell rang and the rest of Fiona's class came in from the playground. They all sat down quietly at their desks.

"Good morning, everyone," said Mr. Moore.

"Good morning, Mr. Moore," they all replied together.

"As you all know, today is another careers day and we have another special guest. I'd like you all to say good morning to Fiona's father, Mr. Stewart."

"Good morning, Mr. Stewart," chorused the children.

"Good morning, everyone. Thank you for inviting me to talk to you. I'm looking forward to it," replied Fiona's father. "I suppose you're wondering what's in all these boxes? Well, you'll know as soon as we get started."

"Mr. Stewart has got something a little different planned for you today," said Mr. Moore. "I think you're all going to find it extremely interesting. Now I'd better let him get started."

Fiona felt a bit better. She liked Mr. Moore, and if he thought it was going to be interesting, then it might just turn out OK.

"Well, as you all know, I'm Fiona's father and I've come to talk to you about my job," her father began. "I'm a paleontologist."

The children all looked puzzled and Fiona started to worry all over again.

"I work at the museum in the city, and I study fossils," he continued. "When people study fossils they can learn more about the different life forms that were around thousands, even millions of years ago."

Fiona sighed – this was just what she had been afraid of. Boring old rocks!

"Does anyone know what a fossil is?" her father asked the children.

"It's a kind of rock," answered John from the back of the room, already sounding very bored. "You study rocks for a job."

Some of the children thought this was funny and began to laugh. Fiona's father studied rocks for a job!

"Now, John," interrupted Mr. Moore, "I know you're excited, but settle down. And that goes for all of you," he said, smiling.

"Well, John," continued Fiona's father, "you're almost right. Do you know anything more about fossils?"

Tom put his hand up.

"A fossil is a part of an animal, like a bone or a shell or something, that has lasted for years and years and years," said Tom.

"That's right," replied Mr. Stewart. "Fossils can also be parts of plants or people. Did you know that a paleontologist called Mary Leakey found some very important fossils in Africa? The fossils were footprints, and they were nearly four million years old."

"Wow," whispered Tom from behind Fiona. He put up his hand once again. "Do you study dinosaur fossils as well?" he asked.

There was a groan from the class. They all knew how much Tom loved dinosaurs.

"Yes, I do," said Mr. Stewart. "I'm very interested in dinosaurs. But I study all kinds of fossils – plant fossils as well as animal ones. But, did you know that dinosaurs aren't the only kind of extinct animal?"

"What's an extinct animal?" asked Sylvia.

"An animal becomes extinct when every one of its kind has died. The only way we can learn about these extinct animals is to study their fossils. Fossils can give us clues as to how they lived, what they ate, and where they lived, of course."

"Why did the dinosaurs become extinct?" asked Tom.

"Yes, I think we'd all like to know more about why dinosaurs became extinct," added Mr. Moore, smiling.

"Well, Tom," said Mr. Stewart, "scientists aren't really sure. Some believe that the weather may have changed, wiping out the food supply. No plants for plant-eating dinosaurs to eat and no other dinosaurs for meat-eaters to eat! Other scientists believe that a huge meteor may have crashed into the earth. This meteor was so big it went right through the earth's crust. It caused huge volcanoes and tidal waves and a big cloud of smoke and ash. The big dark cloud stayed in the sky and changed the weather so much that lots of species couldn't live."

Fiona looked around the classroom. She was surprised to see everyone listening carefully to her father.

"There are some species of animals today that are in danger of becoming extinct," her father continued. "We say that they are endangered."

Sarah put up her hand. "Gorillas are endangered, aren't they?" she asked.

"Yes, they are," replied Mr. Stewart. "Does anyone else know of a species that's endangered?"

John was waving his hand in the air. "Pandas," he said. "I saw them on a nature program. They're big and they eat bamboo and they're endangered!"

Everybody laughed, even Mr. Moore. John didn't usually get excited about answering questions.

"That's very good, and it's important to learn about endangered animals, but today we'll be looking at dinosaurs," said Mr. Stewart.

Tom looked very happy.

"I've got a video here that I made at the museum," said Mr. Stewart. "Some artists and model-makers helped me make it. The video shows what we've learned about dinosaurs from studying fossils. We've learned what they looked like, what they ate, and how they lived."

The World of the Dinosaurs

Everyone waited impatiently while Fiona's father set up the video.

"I think this video could be pretty cool, Fiona," whispered Sheena.

"Do you really think so?" asked Fiona.

The video was called *The World of the Dinosaurs*. Fiona's father had used some of the museum's models and computer pictures of dinosaurs to create different scenes. In one of these scenes, the students felt as if they were watching from the top of a glacier as a group of huge mammoths lumbered past.

Sometimes Mr. Stewart explained something or answered a question. When it was over they all felt a bit strange, as though they had been in a different world.

"Did you see that brachiosaurus? It was huge!" exclaimed Keally.

"I liked the mammoths," said Shelley. "They were like big woolly elephants."

Suddenly it was lunchtime. Everyone was surprised – the morning had gone by very fast.

"OK children, you've had a very interesting morning in the land of the dinosaurs. Go and have your lunch and then we'll see you all back here for our special expedition," said Mr. Moore.

"You're so lucky," said Tom to Fiona, "your father's got such a cool job. I think I might be a paleontologist when I grow up. You get to do all this awesome stuff like dig up fossils and make skeletons of dinosaurs."

"Yeah," said Sheena, "I don't know what you were worried about."

"Neither do I now," replied Fiona. "You just never know with Dad."

The children couldn't wait to get back into the classroom after lunch. As they sat down, they all talked at once, trying to guess where the expedition would take them.

Ready to Dig

"OK, everyone," said Mr. Stewart, "I won't keep you waiting any longer. This afternoon we're going on..." he paused for a minute "...an archeological dig! Now you know why we've asked some parents along to help today."

"Wow!"

"Cool!"

"Awesome!"

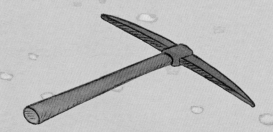

Everyone was talking at once. "What are we going to look for?" asked Sam.

"Well, some people have found fossils very close to the school, so I thought I'd put you children to work to see what you can find," replied Mr. Stewart. "You need to listen to what I say very carefully."

"Right!" shouted John, standing up.

"Wait a minute, John," said Mr. Moore. "All of you, please listen. You'll be divided into groups and each group will be given an area to work in. Nobody is to leave their area without asking first. Now, do you all understand?"

"Yes, Mr. Moore," chorused the students.

"Can we go now?" asked John.

"First I need to explain a few things and give you your equipment," said Mr. Stewart. "The most important thing to remember is that you must be very gentle. Fossils can be millions of years old and they're very fragile. If you find something that you think is a fossil, use these brushes to brush the dirt away very carefully until you can see what you've found."

Mr. Stewart passed the brushes around between the groups and gave each group two small picks. "It's better to use your hand or the brushes, but if the ground is too hard, you may need to loosen it up with the picks. Right? All set?"

"Yes," everyone shouted.

"OK, follow me," said Mr. Stewart, as he and Mr. Moore walked with the students and the parents to the site.

"Here we are. This is the site," said Mr. Stewart. "Mr. Moore's group, you can stay here, and my group will start work over there."

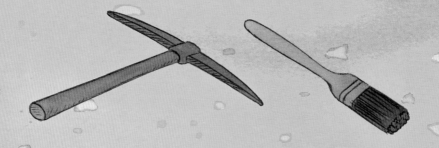

Fiona's Find

Everyone started to sort through the rocks and stones that were lying around, and it wasn't long before John shouted, "I've found one! I've found a fossil!"

"Let's have a look. Bring it over here carefully," said Mr. Stewart. He looked closely at the small piece of rock in John's hand.

"Well, that's a pretty good find, John," he said, "but I'm afraid it's not a genuine fossil."

"What about this one?" asked Tom, coming over.

"Or this?" said Sheena. After that, Mr. Stewart was kept busy for the rest of the afternoon identifying bits of old glass, or small animal bones, but not one fossil.

Then, Fiona turned over a small rock to see if anything was underneath, and something in the rock caught her eye. She looked closer and saw what looked like a dragonfly shape inside the rock. Could this be the real thing? Could it be a fossil?

"What about this, Dad?" she asked, handing the rock to him. He looked at it closely, turning it over and over. Fiona hopped from one foot to the other as she waited for him to make up his mind.

"Congratulations, Fiona," he said finally. "I think we have our first genuine fossil of the day. Maybe I'm not the only paleontologist in the family!"

All the children crowded around to see what Fiona had found. She was pleased with herself but she was even more pleased with her father. She turned around and looked up at him.

"Thanks, Dad," she said. "This has been the best careers day ever!"